SONGS IN THE SHADE OF
THE FLAMBOYANT TREE

FRENCH CREOLE LULLABIES AND NURSERY RHYMES

Aliyèt

GUADELOUPE

Aliette is happy,
her mother is away.
She borrows her dress
and dances.

2 Ti zwazo

HAITI

Little bird,
where are you going?
If you go to Lalo's house,
she will eat you.

3 Toti pa ni dan
HAITI, MARTINIQUE & GUADELOUPE

I dare you to tell me how
the turtle eats without teeth.
I know that you will tell me
sooner or later.

4 Ti train longtemps

REUNION

Do you remember
the little train of yore?
It moved slowly, but happily.

5 Pich mimi

GUADELOUPE

Pinch me, king of misers.
Go away and lay an egg
in your cage.

6 Lè timoun an mwen

GUADELOUPE

Go to sleep,
your daddy is not here.
Your poor mommy
is having a hard time.

6 Manman-doudou

GUADELOUPE

Thanks to your
love Mommy,
we have grown.
We will make you
happy one day.

7 Zinzin

REUNION

Mischief is not a good thing. The egg broke, I swear, it's not my fault.

8 Dodo fillette

GUADELOUPE

Put this child to
sleep until she is
twenty.
If she wakes up,
cut off her ears,
and the little birds
will come to eat
all the pieces.

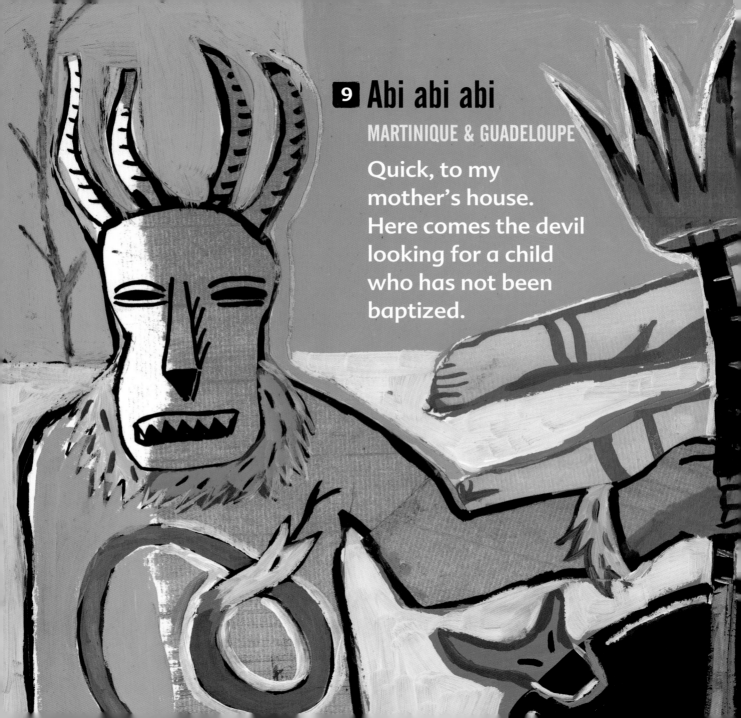

9 Abi abi abi

MARTINIQUE & GUADELOUPE

Quick, to my mother's house. Here comes the devil looking for a child who has not been baptized.

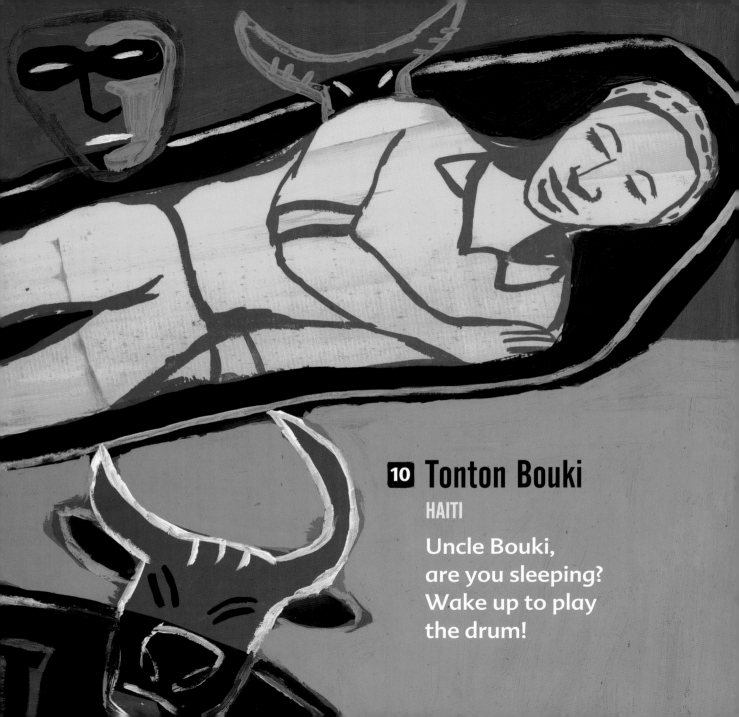

10 Tonton Bouki

HAITI

Uncle Bouki,
are you sleeping?
Wake up to play
the drum!

11 Manman mwen
MARTINIQUE & GUADELOUPE

My mother only gives
me breadfruit every day.
How am I supposed
to put on weight
if she doesn't give
me anything else?

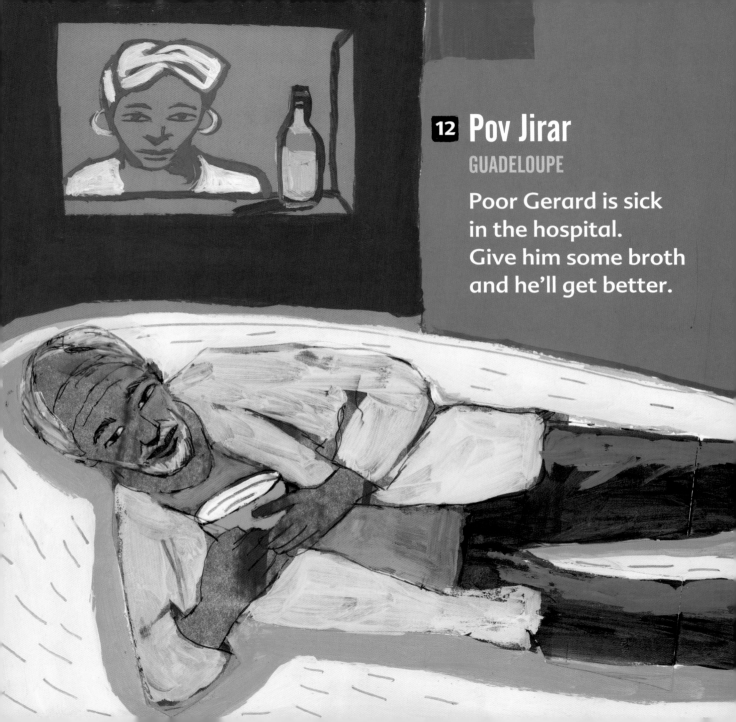

12 Pov Jirar
GUADELOUPE

Poor Gerard is sick in the hospital. Give him some broth and he'll get better.

13 Dlo cho épi kako

GUADELOUPE

How do you make chocolate?
Add some hot water, a bit of cocoa, nutmeg and a bit of coffee!

14 Granmèrkal

REUNION

Grandma Kal,
what time is it? It's midnight,
time to get dressed.
I'm coming to get you.
Here I come !

15 Papiyon volé
MARTINIQUE & GUADELOUPE

Fly butterfly.
All we do is fly.

16 Zizi pan

MARTINIQUE

I'm going out to the point
to look for trouble.
Whether you like it or not.

17 Sat maron

REUNION

As I passed by the ravine,
I found a stray cat.
If the child doesn't
fall asleep, the stray
cat will catch him.

18 P'tit fleur fanée

REUNION

Do you remember
little beloved flower?
We were walking
in the forest.
The birds were singing.
Since then, time
has passed.
All that's left is a
sweet memory.

19 Lapli tonbé

MARTINIQUE & GUADELOUPE

It's raining, it's sunny.
The devil is marrying
his daughter behind
the church.

20 Ban-mwen on ti bo
MARTINIQUE & GUADELOUPE

Who is knocking
at my window?
I have been in the
rain for two hours.
Let me in and give
me a kiss my love
to soothe my heart.

21 Ti somin

REUNION

Narrow path, wide path.
Is the wolf there or not?

22 Yaya, Tiwowo é Banda

HAITI

They went to the river
to catch some fish.
Mother warned them.
It's not time to rest.

23 Solda ka kaka

GUADELOUPE

Soldiers do it
standing up.
It's for glory,
my dear.

24 Zélèv lékol
HAITI

School children, get up.
Don't get discouraged.

25 Mabèl-o
MARTINIQUE

Pretty one,
cut the bottom,
cut the top,
remove the leaves.
A lovely cane indeed

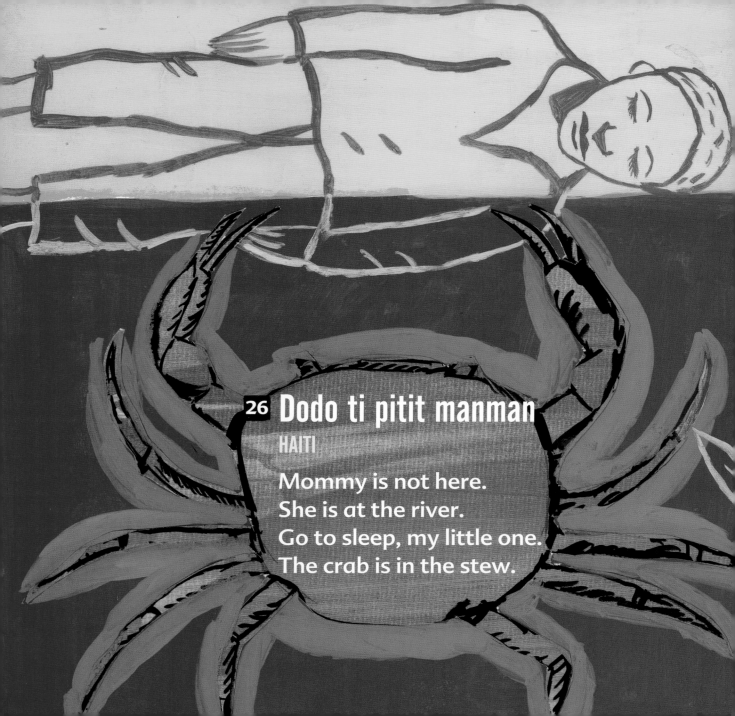

26 Dodo ti pitit manman
HAITI

Mommy is not here.
She is at the river.
Go to sleep, my little one.
The crab is in the stew.

27 Dodo la minèt

REUNION

Go to sleep sweet child.
If she doesn't, the stray
cat will catch her.

28 Lari Zabim

MARTINIQUE & GUADELOUPE

Behind the old lady's straw hut,
there was a pepper plant.
The old lady got very hot
and it killed the plant!

29 Zandoli mandé mayé

MARTINIQUE & GUADELOUPE

One small lizard proposes marriage. The other answers: no, no, no.

30 Adyé foula
GUADELOUPE

Goodbye scarves
and necklaces.
My darling is gone.
His ship has left
forever.

About the songs

The traditional Creole children's repertoire is very colourful. Gathered from parents who grew up in Haiti, Guadeloupe, Martinique and Reunion Island, the 30 nursery rhymes are also often found in Guyana and Mauritius.

Along with nursery rhymes are love songs and work songs that recount the history of the Creole people using a variety of historical references. Others, which are more focused on the relationships between men and women, are meant to be humourous and can involve both children and grown-ups. Certain nursery rhymes also use elements of the French repertory while incorporating aspects typically found in the Creole world: mysterious animals, devils and characters with magical or evil powers, flavours, spices, traditional dishes and foods... As in all cultures, some rhymes are used to bounce children on one's lap, to swing them, to play tag, dance and laugh together.

The lullabies are superb and often capture the difficulties in raising children when money and emotional stability are in short supply. This landscape would not be complete without references to celebrations and carnivals that bring together all the generations around improvised songs. Accompanied by all sorts of percussion instruments (piker, ti bwa, kayamb, bélé drum, rouleur...); also by the bobre (musical bow), the bamboo flute, the accordion, the banjo and the piano, maloya and sega coexist here with mazurka or biguine.

1 Aliyèt (Aliette) GUADELOUPE

Singer **Roselaine Bicep**

Aliyèt kontan manman-y pa la	Aliette is happy, mother is not there
I dansé on ti penm penm pen lenm	She dances a little penm penm pen lenm
Aliyèt kontan manman-y pa la	Aliette is happy, mother is not there
I mété chapo a gran ribò	She puts on a wide-brimmed hat
I mété wòb a gran volan	She puts on a ruffled dress
I mété jip a gran volan	She puts on a ruffled skirt
I mété jipon a gran dantèl	She puts on a lace petticoat
I mété soulyé a gran talon	She puts on high-heel shoes

What little girl hasn't dressed up in her mother's clothes to look like her and feel like a grown-up? Here, while her mother is away, little Aliette (a typical old-fashioned Creole name, like Avriette, Monette, Henriette or Mariette) gets all decked out in the big hat, the dress, the skirt, the petticoat and, of course, the high-heel shoes. You can imagine her dancing away in front of the mirror! The song can also be continued and varied by adding other accessories to the list.

2 **Ti zwazo (Little Bird)** HAITI
Singers **Roselaine Bicep, Claudette Thégat**

Ti zwazo koté ou pralé
Mwen pralé kay fiyèt Lalo
Fiyèt Lalo konn manjé timoun
Si ou alé l'a manjé ou tou
Brikolobrik brikolobrik
Rosignol manjé kòròsòl
Ay roulo roulo roulo an sòtann lavil Léogàn
Tou bèt tonbé nan bwa
Madmwazèl lévé pou dansé
Mesyeu mwen fatigé

Koulèv tonbé nan bwa
Mabouya tonbé nan bwa
Zandoli tonbé nan bwa
Kwapo tonbé nan bwa

Little bird, where are you going?
I'm going to little Lalo's house
Little Lalo eats children
If you go there, she will eat you too
Brikolobrik brikolobrik
The nightingale eats the soursop*
Ow! Go fast fast fast when leaving the city of Léogan
All the creatures of the forest have fallen
Young lady, come dance!
Sir, I am tired!

The grass snake fell in the forest
The mabouya* fell in the forest
The anoli* fell in the forest
The toad fell in the forest

* Soursop: exotic fruit with a very tasty juice
* Mabouya and anoli: small lizards

Passed down from generation to generation, this song is frequently sung at home or in the schoolyard by 6 and 7-year-olds. This nursery rhyme uses a cheerful dialogue to warn of the dangers of certain encounters (witches, threatening animals, and so on). The advice lavished onto this little bird provides an opportunity to introduce children to the world around them, inhabited by lizards (including the worrisome iguana) and toads, among other things.

3 **Tóti pa ni dan (The turtle eats without teeth)** HAITI, MARTINIQUE & GUADELOUPE
Singers **Dédé Saint-Prix, Tali Boumandil, Juliette Hoarau**

Tòti pa ni dan laten di mwen ki sa i ké manjé
Woy woy woy ou a di-mwen ki sa i ké manjé

I dare you to tell me how the turtle eats without teeth
Woy woy woy, you'll eventually tell me how it eats

This rhythmical nursery rhyme is sung by both adults and children. Sung in unison on the way to school, it once again evokes the mysterious animal world, in which the turtle plays an important role both in nature and in the world of fantasy. It is found in fairytales and proverbs such as *Tortue y trouve pas son qué* (You cannot achieve something that is impossible). A Haitian version exists that is sung to a slightly different melody. On the bamboo flute, a traditional instrument of Martinique, the musician Dédé Saint-Prix weaves an airy tune to the rhythms of the bélé drums.

4 Ti train longtemps (The little train of yore) REUNION

Singer **Daniéla Rossignol** Songwriter **Jules Joron**

Di à moin si ti connais comment té y fé
le ti train longtemps ôté
La picapab' picapab' picapab' jusqu'à
la gare Saint-Louis
Tiou tiou tiou tiou !
Lité y march' douc'ment mais quand
mêm' ça lité content

Tell me if you know what the train of old sounded like
La picapab' picapab' picapab' all the way to Saint-Louis station
Tiou tiou tiou tiou !
It moved slowly, but it was still happy

The arrival of the railroad profoundly marked the popular imagination. In several countries (Brazil, Germany, France, etc.) songs or nursery rhymes can be found that invite children to form a little train and sway to the rhythm of the song. This song is accompanied by the kayamb: a large, flat maraca made of sugar cane flower stems and filled with various grains that produce a very particular sound when they slide. You can also hear the rouleur, a large drum covered with cow hide fastened to a rum barrel, and the bobre, a musical bow with a calabash attached to it that acts as a resonator, played with a little bamboo stick. In Reunion, these various instruments have contributed to the creation of maloya. This music, with African and Madagascan roots, expressed the daily joys and suffering of slaves in Reunion. Banned for a long time, maloya has remained a vessel for feelings of rebellion and protest, and continues today to broach serious topics, such as war, racism, the environment, and so on. The author of this song has performed countless popular pieces of sega (such as "A cause Fifine" and "Voleur canard"), a genre similar to maloya.

5 Pich mimi (Pinch me) GUADELOUPE

Singer **Marie-Paule Dantin**

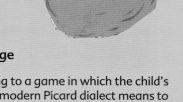

Pich mimi
Wa dépeng
Vatan ponn dan ta kalòj
Vatan dir a mon konpè
Danvwayé on ti poulé
Tou cho
Tou fwa
Vatan ponn dan ta kalòj

Pinch me
King of misers
Go away and lay an egg in your cage
Go away and tell my buddy
To send a little chicken
Nice and hot
Nice and cold
Go away and lay an egg in your cage

This nursery rhyme collected by Marie-Christine Hazaël-Massieux in Guadeloupe is sung along to a game in which the child's hand is squeezed to the rhythm of the song. It likely originated in Picardy, France. "Pincher" in modern Picard dialect means to pinch or steal, and giving a kiss "à l'pinchette" means to kiss your child while pinching her or his cheeks. Also, the term "kaloj" (cage) can be linked to "gayolle" or "cayolle" (also meaning cage). "Ti poulé" in Creole is "tchot poulet" in Picard.

6   Lè timoun an mwen (My child) GUADELOUPE
Singer **Roselaine Bicep**

Lè pitit an-mwen ka mandé-mwen tété
Mwen kalé ba-li manjé matété
Dodo pitit, papa pa la
Sé manman tousèl ki dan lanbara
Dodo pitit, papa pa la
Sé manman tousèl ki dan la miser

When my child asks to nurse
I give him matété* to eat
Go to sleep, baby, daddy is not here
Mommy is all alone, she's having a hard time
Go to sleep, baby, daddy is not here
Mommy is alone, she is very poor

* Matété: sweet porridge of bread and milk

The theme of the wife abandoned by her husband is recurrent in songs from the islands. Lullabies often provide an opportunity for the mother to open up and to ease her own fears. This song, which plays with the tones of words, has various versions. Depending on the circumstances, the husband may be gone fishing or to the city, always leaving his wife in charge of the child and the house. When the child cries, the mother doesn't always know what to say. Here, since he wants to nurse, she offers him matété, a dish consisting of rice and crab that is obviously not suitable for the baby.

6   Manman-doudou (Dear Mommy) GUADELOUPE
Singer **Roselaine Bicep** Lyricist **Ektò Poulé**

Aprédavwa manman nou ban-nou tété
I viré ban-nou manjé matété
Manman-doudou evè lanmou
Ou rivé fè si nou gran jòdijou
E si dèmen manman-nou bizwen tété
Nou ké sav ba-li manjé matété
Manman-doudou ou pé kwè-nou
Nou ké sav fè ou kontan nou on jou
Nou pa té ké vlé dèmen ou règrété
Lè nou té piti ou ban-nou tété
Manman-doudou si lavi dou
Sé davwa on jou ou fè-nou vwè jou

After mother has nursed us
Now she gives us matété
Dear mommy, thanks to your love
You have allowed us to grow, right up until today
And if tomorrow our mother needs to be nursed
We will know to give her matété
Dear mommy, you can believe us
We will make you happy one day
We don't want you to ever regret
Nursing us when we were little
Dear mommy, if life is sweet
It's because you gave us life one day

The verses, written by Hector Poullet, bring a new meaning to the wonderful melody of "Lè timoun an mwen". After the harshness, the Guadelupian writer offers a message of solidarity: The adult children now offer their affection and support to their ageing parents.

7 **Zinzin** REUNION
Singer **Daniéla Rossignol**

Zinzin, la malis la pa bon	Zinzin, mischief is not a good thing
Me z'oeuf la kasé, la pa moin lotèr	The egg broke, it is not my fault
You !	Wow !

In this game played in pairs, children face each other and pile their four hands on top of each other, each hand lightly squeezing the one beneath. In this hold, they move them up and down to the rhythm of the nursery rhyme. On the final "You" they let go. This can also be played with several people in a circle, building a pyramid of hands, which makes it more fun as the pyramid grows in size.

8 **Dodo fillette (Go to sleep little girl)** GUADELOUPE
Singer **Lucienne Samson**

Dodo fillette	Go to sleep, little girl
Sainte-Elisabeth	Saint Elisabeth
Endormez-moi cette enfant	Put this child to sleep for me
Jusqu'à l'âge de vingt ans	Until she is twenty
Si elle se réveille	If she wakes up
Cupez-lui l'oreille	Cut off her ear
Et les p'tits oiseaux viendront	And the little birds will come
Pour manger tous les morceaux	To eat all the pieces
Do oui dodo	Sleep, yes, sleep
C'est maman qui l'a dit	Because mommy said so
Do oui dodo	Sleep, yes, sleep
C'est papa qui l'a dit	Because daddy said so
Dododo pitit a manman	Sleep, my little one
Si pitit an-mwen vlé pa dodo	If my baby won't sleep
Gro dyab-la ké vini pran-y	The big devil will take her away

This lullaby, also sung in Guyana, has French verses and a Creole chorus that is actually very similar to the Haitian lullaby "Dodo ti pitit manman". Variants of this lullaby can be found in many regions of France: "Dodo Béline", "Néné petite", "Dodo petite", which all summon a saint (Catherine or Marguerite) as a protective figure to lull the child to sleep. There are no threats, but rather the promise of a marriage to Pierrot, a nice boy, in the French version below.

Dodo petite (Go to sleep, little girl)	Il faudra la marier (She will have to be married)
Sainte Marguerite (Saint Marguerite)	Dans une chambre (In a room)
Endormez-moi mon enfant (Make my child fall asleep)	Pleine d'amandes (Full of almonds)
Quand quinze ans auront sonné (Until the age of fifteen)	Un mortier pour les casser (A mortar to break them)
	Et Pierrot pour le manger (And Pierrot to eat them)

Abi abi abi MARTINIQUE & GUADELOUPE
Singer **Lucienne Samson**

Abi abi abi kay manman	Abi abi abi... quick, to my mother's house
Mi dyab-la déwò	Here comes the devil
Dyab-la ka mandé an ti manmay	The devil is looking for a child
An ti manmay ki san batenm	A child who has not been baptized

This French antillean biguine is mostly sung on Mardi gras during the carnival in Martinique. That day, the whole population wears masks and devil costumes. In doing so, they trick him and therefor protect themselves from him. By ridiculing him, they tame him by creating this red swarm of people hurtling through the towns and villages to the beat of drums. On the recording, there's a Jamaican steel drum, a hammered pan that produces a range of metallic sounds also found in Martinique.

 ## Tonton Bouki (Uncle Bouki) HAITI
Singers **Dormélia Bénédict, Claudette Thégat**

Tonton Bouki	Uncle Bouki
Ou ap dòmi ?	Are you sleeping?
Lévé pou bat tanbou-a	Wake up to play the drum!
Ding ding dong !	Ding ding dong !
Kili kili an pou al nan siléma	Kili kili, I have to go to the movies

"Uncle Bouki" is a take on "Frère Jacques" ("Brother John") in which "Sonnez les matines" ("Morning bells are ringing") becomes "Wake up to play the drum." Bouki is said to have originally been one of the two heroes of an African epic poem and the equivalent of Isengrin in the Roman de Renart. He has a cousin in Guadeloupe: Compèr Zanba, a character that always gets duped by a rabbit. The end of the nursery rhyme, "Kili kili, I have to go to the movies," seems to be a more recent broad interpretation.

11 Manman mwen (My mother) MARTINIQUE & GUADELOUPE
Singer **Marie-Paule Dantin**

Manman mwen ki fè diridou
I ba Nikola
I pa ba mwen adan
Touléjou sé lafarin sèch
Lanmori woti
Epi fouyapen
Ki mannyè ou lé mwen vini gwo
Si manman mwen pa ka ba mwen manjé
Ki mannyè ou lé mwen vini gwo
Si manman mwen pa ka ba mwen ayen

My mother made rice pudding
She gave some to Nicholas
But not to me
Every day it is dry meal
Roast cod
And then breadfruit*
How am I supposed to put on weight
If my mother doesn't feed me?
How am I supposed to put on weight
If my mother doesn't give me anything?

* Breadfruit: fruit of the bread tree, used as a vegetable

This well-known lullaby that is greatly enjoyed by mothers in Martinique, Guadeloupe, and Guyana expresses the poverty that affects young children. Breadfruit is a starchy vegetable accessible to all. In periods of food shortage, it makes for an inexpensive meal along with a bit of cod and oil.

12 Pov Jirar (Poor Gerard) GUADELOUPE
Singers **Lucienne Samson, Terri Samson**

Pov Jirar
Jirar malad
A lopital
Ba-li bouyon
Ba-li mader
Li ké géri !

Poor Gerard
Gerard is sick
In the hospital
Give him some broth
Give him some madère*
So that he gets better!

* Madère: drink or tuber that tastes like potato or chestnut, cooked in water, fried or mashed.

In this game, the child sits on the adult's lap, they hold hands and the adult rocks the child back and forth. On "Li ké géri," the child is tipped upside down.

13 Dlo cho épi kako (Hot water and cocoa) GUADELOUPE

Singers **Josette Césarin, Paul Mindy**

Dlo cho épi kako	Hot water and cocoa
Comment fait-on le chocolat?	How do you make chocolate?
Dlo cho épi kako	Hot water and cocoa
Yo ka mété miskad adan-y	Add some nutmeg
Dlo cho épi kako	Hot water and cocoa
Yo ka mété tibwen kako	Add a bit of cocoa
Dlo cho épi kako	Hot water and cocoa
Yo ka mété tibwen kafé...	Add a bit of coffee...

The cacao tree (pyé-kako), a central theme of this nursery rhyme, grows in the Caribbean and produces a fruit whose highly valued seed played a significant role in the colonial economy. In Martinique, on the morning of their first communion, children would enjoy a breakfast of hot chocolate thickened over low heat and flavoured with cinnamon, nutmeg and lime zest.

Like "Papiyon volé", this nursery rhyme is also frequently sung during trips, family celebrations and the carnival. A leader is asked in unison about the various ways to flavour chocolate. The leader answers and doesn't hesitate to digress—about a local event, people present, etc.—or to make more suggestive innuendos with a double entendre. The interpretation adopted in this recording, at any rate, is definitely suggestive of mockery and dancing.

14 Granmèrkal (Grandma Kal) REUNION

Voices **Daniéla Rossignol, Micheline Tamachia**

Granmèrkal kél hèr i lé ?	Grandma Kal, what time is it?
In èr !	One o'clock!
Dé zèr !	Two o'clock!
Minui ! Mi arriv !	Midnight! Here I come!
Granmèrkal, kosa ou pou fé ? (repeated)	Grandma Kal, what are you doing?
Mi mèt mon kabay	I'm putting on my shirt
Mi mèt mon zupe	I'm putting on my skirt
Mi mèt mon sokèt	I'm putting on my socks
Mi mèt mon soulié	I'm putting on my shoes
Mi égiz mon kouto	I'm sharpening my knife
A la, mi vien ! Haaaaaa !	Here I come! Aaaaaah!

Like the French nursery rhyme "Promenons-nous dans les bois" (in which children anticipate and then run from the scary wolf), this nursery rhyme played mainly by 6 to 8-year-olds in Reunion is used to brave danger and scare each other. The character of Granmèrkal owes her legendary status to a certain madame Desbasseyns, who was born in 1755 and died in 1846. After the death of her husband, she ruled over 500 hectares and 400 slaves for 45 years, on one of the largest properties on the island. Known by notables as an extremely efficient and level-headed woman, she was feared by the slaves. She died two years before the abolition of slavery, and her image has remained associated with that of a witch. Legends remain today that associate her with a volcano: "Madame Desbasseyns la réveillé et li lé en colère," (Madame Desbasseyns woke it up and it is angry) or "Quand l'volcan i ronfle, Madame Desbasseyns i gagne coup d'chabouk; li demande pardon" (When the volcano snores, Madame Desbasseyns gets the whip; she asks for forgiveness)." The character of Granmèrkal was even revived recently to thwart the import of Halloween!

15 Papiyon volé (Fly butterfly) MARTINIQUE & GUADELOUPE
Singer Josette Césarin

Papiyon volé	Fly butterfly
Sé volé nou ka volé	All we do is fly

A true Caribbean classic, the chorus "Papiyon volé" can be sung collectively in various circumstances: trips, weddings, balls, and so on. During the carnival, it is performed along with other songs to lead the vidés (parades), and a leader improvises various verses to the rhythm of the snare drum. Other, slightly different melodies also exist. "Papiyon volé" is also a musical and psychomotor game for children. The lyrics are varied ("Papiyon zouké," etc.) and hands are crossed to make them fly, dance, jump, turn, rock and, finally, land.

16 Zizi pan MARTINIQUE
Singers Dédé Saint-Prix, Tali Boumandil, Juliettte Hoarau

Zizi pan pan pan pan	Zizi pan pan pan pan
Mwen kalé lapwent aché makanda	I'm going to Pointe-à-Pitre to look for trouble
Ki ou vlé ki ou vlé pas	Whether you like it or not
Mwen kalé lapwent aché makanda	I'm going to Pointe-à-Pitre to look for trouble

This nursery rhyme accompanies a war dance in which everyone stands in a circle and claps their hands. In the centre, two children face each other. One of them taps a stick to the rhythm, while the other passes his or her hand underneath, trying not to get hit. The children singing the nursery rhyme in unison have fun braving danger. In the past, during funeral wakes, the object was to spread your fingers apart fast enough to avoid a large kitchen knife. It should be noted that the piano arrived on the Caribbean music scene to accompany quadrilles, mazurkas and waltzes in the 19th century. In this case, it adds another dimension musically speaking, by being associated with the ti-bwa and piker (wood and bamboo percussion instruments).

17 Sat maron (The stray cat) REUNION

Singer **Micheline Tamachia**

An pasan la ravine Saint-Gilles
Moin la trouv in vié gramoun
Mi d'mand ali kouk li fé la
Li di amoin la pès kabo

As I passed by the Saint-Gilles ravine
I found an old man
I asked him what he was doing there
He said: "I'm fishing sand smelt"

Ouail-ouail mon zanfan
Fo travay po gagn son pin
An pasan la ravine Saint-Gilles
Moin la trouv in sat maron
Si lanfan i dodo pa
Sat maron va souk ali

Hey-hey, my child
You have to work to earn your bread
As I passed by the Saint-Gilles ravine
I found a stray cat
If a child doesn't fall asleep
The stray cat will catch him

This lullaby features the stray cat. The word "marron" comes from the Spanish "cimarrón," which means to run away and originally referred to domesticated animals that became feral again. In French, its meaning was even expanded to refer to runaway slaves. Hence, maroons were descendants of slaves who had escaped from cities and taken refuge high in the mountains. They lived in villages built in difficult-to-access cirques in Cilaos, Mafate or Salazie. This lullaby mentions the ravine located near Saint-Gilles, on the west coast of Reunion. Ravines designate the many deep recesses found on the island that are often places where children play or lovers meet. The old man featured in this song is fishing sand smelt. This term is used to describe several sea or river fish, such as the kabo soter, a small black fish that jumps on the rocks and can remain out of water for a long time. A variant of this lullaby can also be found in Mauritius.

18 P'tit fleur fanée (Little wilted flower) REUNION

Singers Daniéla Rossignol, Micheline Tamachia **Songwriters** Georges Fourcade (lyrics), Jules Fossy (music)

Vi souviens mon nénère adoré
Le p'tit bouquet que vous la donne à moin
Na longtemps qu'li lé fané
Si vi souviens comm' ça l'est loin

Do you remember, my sweet darling
The little bouquet you gave me?
It wilted long ago
Do you remember? It was so long ago

P'tit' fleur fanée, p'tit' fleur aimée
Di à moin toujours, kouk c'est l'amour
Vi marchais dans la forêt
Y faisait bon y faisait frais
Dann z'herbe l'avait la rosée
Dans le ciel z'oiseaux y chantaient

Little wilted flower, little beloved flower
Tell me always, what love is
We were walking in the forest
It was nice, it was cool
In the grass, there was dew
In the sky, the birds were singing

Depuis ça le temps l'a passé
Y reste plus qu'un doux souvenir
Quand mi pense mon coeur l'est brisé
Tout' ici ba comme ça y doit finir

Since then, time has passed
All that's left is a sweet memory
When I think about it, my heart breaks
As everything down here must come to an end

It is said that if Reunion were to become independent, this love song would be its national anthem. With intense, moving and nostalgic character, it eases the country's pain and might be sung even more frequently abroad in France for instance than on the island. It brings together young and old, who sway together arm in arm as you would to a sea shanty. Countless versions exist for the simple reason that most if not all Reunion singers include it in their repertory.

19 Lapli tonbé (It's raining) MARTINIQUE & GUADELOUPE

Singer Roselaine Bicep

Lapli tonbé
Solèy lévé
Dyab ka mayé fi a-y dèyè légliz

It's raining
It's sunny
It's the devil marrying his daughter behind the church!

It is a surprising but true fact that rain and sun go hand in hand! This paradox is reinforced by this equally incongruous story of the devil marrying his daughter, behind the church, no less. Sung each time the sun comes out while it is raining, this nursery rhyme also accompanies a circle dance in which the children have fun varying the rhythms. The lyrics are in Martinique Creole.

20 Ban-mwen on ti bo (Give me a kiss) MARTINIQUE & GUADELOUPE

Singers Marie-Paule Dantin, Lucienne Samson **Lyricist** Armand Siobud (1865–1943)

Toc-toc, toc-toc !	Knock, knock !
Qui frappe à ma fenêtre !	Who's knocking at my window
Sé mwen lanmou	It is I, my love
Sé mwen pen-dou sikré	It is I, your sweet warm bread
Dèpi dézè	For two hours
Lapli ka mouyé-mwen	I have been in the rain
Pa pityé, pa imanité	For pity's sake, for humanity's sake
Wouvè lapòt-la ban-mwen	Open the door and let me in
Ban-mwen on ti bo, dé ti bo,	Give me one kiss, two kisses,
Twa ti bo doudou	Three kisses, my dear
Ban-mwen on ti bo, dé ti bo,	Give me one kiss, two kisses,
Twa ti bo lanmou	Three kisses, my love
Ban-mwen on ti bo, dé ti bo,	Give me one kiss, two kisses,
Twa ti bo	Three kisses
Ban-mwen tousa ou vlé,	Give me as many as you like
Pou soulagé kyè mwen	To soothe my heart
Mwen ka travay	I work
Si jou dan la simenn	Six days a week
Twa jou pou mwen	Three days for me
Twa jou pou doudou-mwen	Three days for my darling
Sanmdi rivé	But Saturday is here
Béké pa ka péyé-mwen	The béké* hasn't paid me
Tifi-la pwan pwagna	She took the dagger
Pou-li pwagnawdé-mwen	To stab me
Quand tu iras	When you go
Un jour au cimetier'	One day to the cemetery
Tu trouveras	You will find
Trois pierres gravées à mon nom	Three stones with my name engraved on them
Sur ces trois pierres	On these three stones
Trois petites fleurs fanées	Three little wilted flowers
La plus fanée des trois	The most wilted of the three
C'est mon coeur oublié par toi	Is my heart forgotten by you

* Béké: wealthy white man, in this case the boss

This song conveys important themes such as love, work and death. In this tragic tale, the "béké" (the White boss in Martinique, equivalent to the "blanc pays" in Guadeloupe) has not paid for the work done. The piano performance by Mario Canonge brilliantly revives this revered classic from the Lesser Antilles.

21 Ti somin (Little path) REUNION

Singers **Daniéla Rossignol, Micheline Tamachia**

Ti somin gran somin	Little path, big path
Le lou lé la ou pa la ?	Is the wolf there or not?
Pa la !	Not there!
Ti somin gran somin	Little path, big path
Lé la !	He's here!
Guili guili !	Tickle tickle!

This question-and-answer nursery rhyme is used as soon as the child begins to speak. As in the French "La petite bête qui monte", the index and middle fingers slowly creep (walk) up the child's arm, stopping to see if the wolf is there. If he is there, the fingers turn back and start again from the beginning. If he is not there, they move up and tickle the child under the arm or on the neck.

22 Yaya, Tiwowo é Banda (Yaya, Tiroro and Banda) HAITI

Singers **Dormélia Bénédict, Claudette Thégat**

Yaya, Tiwowo é Banda	Yaya, Li'l Roro and Banda
L'alé larivyè l'al péché pwason	Went to the river to catch some fish
Manman di konsa	Mother warned them
Si' w pa fè'l l'a kalé-w	That if they don't do it, they'll be beaten
Mézanmi !	My friends!
Ba-li'l alaso !	Go, get to it!
Si koté	To the side
An mitan	In the middle
Dèyè-do	Turn your back
Toutouk-touk !	Toutouk-touk !
Si ou pa kovèk	If you're not up to it
Pa vini chita son sa	Don't come here to rest

This song performed by girls or boys accompanies a dance for two. The mother asks her daughter Yaya and her brothers to go fishing. The moral is straightforward: if you want to eat, you have to work. But the children do not listen to her; they dance around in a circle, once to the right, then to the left, in the middle and turning their backs, explicitly mimicking a seduction game. The musical arrangement showcases the bells and bass drums found in voodoo and trance music. The intermingled sounds of the panpipe (made from bottles) and the friction drum add to the mystery of the song.

23 Solda ka kaka (Soldiers poop) GUADELOUPE

Singer **Lucienne Samson, Terri Samson**

Solda ka kaka tou doubout
Sé pou loné a yo chè
Solda ka kaka tou doubout
Sé pou loné a yo

Soldiers poop standing up
It's for glory, my dear
Soldiers poop standing up
It's for glory

Often beginning with "ta ta ta ta" sounds that imitate a fire station siren, this nursery rhyme sung to little children pokes fun at soldiers. It is similar to a riddle, a popular genre of the Creole oral tradition. Another response to the question "Why do soldiers poop standing up?" ("Solda ka kaka tou doubout?") is "Bougi!" (a burning candle). You can also hear the following:

Dio doubout (Why is water standing up ?)
Kann (Sugar cane)

Dlo pann (Why has the water stopped?)
Koko (Coconut)

In regard to the soldiers who poop standing up, there is also a proverb that goes "Sòlda ka kaka tou doubout, sè pou lonnè a-yo (If soldiers go in their boots, it's to save their honour)." In other words, hard times call for drastic measures!

24 Zélèv lékol (The school children) HAITI

Singers **Dormélia Bénédict, Claudette Thégat**

Zélèv lékol
Pat espéré sil ta mété pontalé gogo
Sat pa ka viré
Lévé li pa ra bi

The school children
Did not hope to one day wear bloomers
Even if you can't twirl
Get up, don't get discouraged

A highly symbolic and desired garment, the "culotte à gogo," an undergarment trimmed with lace flounces, worn by little schoolgirls who make no bones about spinning their skirt to show it off. The nursery rhyme tells those who do not wear one not to be ashamed of it. Sung at the end of the school day in Haitian schools, it knows many variants and interpretations, with an ironic portrayal of the interactions between rich and poor. It is customary in Haiti for schoolchildren to be impeccably dressed. School is not free, and families make sacrifices to enrol their children and provide the necessities, including the illustrious "culotte à gogo." Unfortunately, many children are, in fact, not sent to school.

25 Mabèl-o (Oh my lovely) MARTINIQUE

Singers Dédé Saint-Prix, Tali Boumandil, Juliette Hoarau

Mabèl-o mabèl-o	My lovely, oh my lovely
Zip zap wabap	Cut the bottom, cut the top, remove the leaves
Mabèl-o kèl joli kanno mabèl-o	My lovely, what a nice cane, my lovely
Zip zap wabap	Cut the bottom, cut the top, remove the leaves
Man ka travay trasé	I plough
Man ka mennen kabouwé	I drive the cart
Man ba Jéjé lajan	I gave Jéjé money
Jéjé ka kòné mwen toujou	She still cheated on me
Way Jéjé siwo la	Ah, this syrup, Jéjé
Siwo-la siwo-la siwo-la Jéjé	This syrup, this syrup, this syrup, Jéjé
Way Jéjé siwo la	Ah, this syrup, Jéjé
Siwo tala pa bon pou mwen	Ah, this syrup is not good for me
Doumbélédoum bélédoum manman tonbé	Boom bada boom, it spilled
Viré météy adan-y	Put it back in
Zouma zouma zoum manman tonbé	Zoom zoom zoom, it spilled
Viré météy adan-y...	Put it back in...

This is a work song that helped sugar cane cutters keep up the pace. Banned for several years, this dance has become a classic of the folklore repertory. The pretty cane cutter goes "zip" with her knife to cut the base of the cane, "zap" to cut the top and "wabap" to remove the leaves. Children sing the song while imitating the actions of the cutters.

26 Dodo ti pitit manman (Go to sleep little Mommy) HAITI

Singer Claudette Thégat

Dodo ti pitit manman	Go to sleep my little one
Manman-w ou pa la	Mommy is not here
L'alé larivyè	She is at the river
Si ou pa dodo djab la va manjé-w	If you don't go to sleep, the devil will eat you
Dodo pitit krab nan kalalou	Go to sleep, little one, the crab is in the calalou

This lullaby is popular in Haiti and is also sung in Guadeloupe. The devil or crab threatens the child who doesn't want to go to sleep. Creole children are very familiar with crabs as they are common in their environment. Many different varieties can be found there: sea crabs, such as touloulous, siriks, crababarbes, and also large land crabs that live in the woods and are grilled to eat. As for the nan kalalou crab featured in the song, it is cooked with green leaves (madé leaves) or spinach and a side of lard.

27 Dodo la minèt (Sleep little girl) REUNION
Singer **Micheline Tamachia**

Dodo la minèt	Go to sleep sweetie
Lanfan de Janèt	Child of Jeannette
Si la minèt i dodo pa	If the sweet child doesn't go to sleep
Sat maron va souk ali	The stray cat will catch her

Once again, as in the songs "Dodo fiyèt" or "Sat maron", children are threatened to make them go to sleep: little carnivorous birds and the devil in Guadeloupe, the crab in Haiti, the illustrious stray cat in Reunion, and so on. Singing threats in a gentle and calm way is also an outlet for the adult, whose patience has sometimes run thin.

28 Lari Zabim (Rue des Abîmes) MARTINIQUE & GUADELOUPE
Singers **Marie-Paule Dantin, Lucienne Samson**

Lari Zabim té ni on vyé madanm	There was an old lady on Rue des Abîmes
Vyé madanm-la té ni on kaz an pay	The old lady lived in a straw hut
Dèyè kaz-la té ni on pyé piman	And behind her hut, there was a pepper plant
Chalè a vyé fanm-la	And the heat from this old lady
Tyouyé pyé piman-la chè	Was so strong that it killed the pepper plant
La la la la...	If you can believe it!
	La la la la...

This song with a mazurka rhythm is sung in unison in the streets during festivals or carnivals. Rue Des Abymes is none other than Rue Frébault, the main street of Pointe-à-Pitre, but the song is also sung in Martinique and Guyana. The lyrics compare the warm weather to the heat of a pepper and to the character of a woman with quite a reputation! Straw huts were home to the poorest families right up until the 1970s, and pepper trees, as well as lemon trees, spring onion plants, and medicinal plants were often found in their yards.

The banjo on the recording is an instrument that was played throughout the Caribbean, particularly during carnivals. It has the advantage of being very resonant, so that it is not drowned out by the numerous percussion instruments. As for the piano, it was widely used for ballroom dancing and became a mainstay of the a part of the West Indies musical scene.

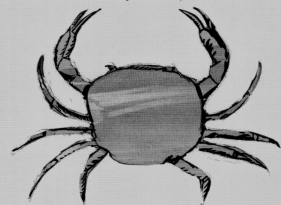

Zandoli mandé mayé (Anoli proposes marriage) MARTINIQUE & GUADELOUPE
Singer **Dédé Saint-Pirx**

Zandoli mandé mayé
Mabouya says no no no

Anoli* proposes marriage
Mabouya* says no no no

* Mabouya and anoli: small lizards

This nursery rhyme features two animals thought to have magical powers: the anoli, a green lizard that only comes out in the day, and the mabouya, a grey lizard that only comes out at night. Zandoli wants to marry Mabouya, but the latter refuses because they will never be able to enjoy life together. The melody mimics the sound of the bells that ring when the newlyweds leave the church. Actually, when children pretend that they or their dolls are getting married, one of them imitates the bell ringer by pulling on a rope tied to a tree, which represents the church. In Martinique, mothers also lull their children to sleep by singing this song very slowly. A bamboo flute accompanies the song.

30 Adyé foula (Goodbye scarves) GUADELOUPE

Singer **Josette Césarin**

Adyé foula, adyé madras
Adyé grendò, adyé kolyéchou
Doudou an-mwen i ka pati
Élas, élas, sé pou toujou
Bonjou misyé lè kapitèn
Boujou misyé lè komandan
Mwen vini fè on ti pétisyon
Pou yo lésé doudou an-mwen banmwen

Mademoiselle il est trop tard
La consigne est déjà signée
Doudou a-vou i ka pati
Le navire est sur la bouée
Adyé foula, adyé madras
Adyé grendò, adyé kolyéchou
Doudou an-mwen i ka pati
Élas, élas, sé pou toujou

Goodbye scarves, goodbye madras
Goodbye grain d'or*, goodbye collier chou*
My darling is gone
Alas, alas, it is forever
Hello Captain
Hello Commander
I have come to make a plea
For my darling to stay with me

It is too late, Miss
The order is already signed
Your darling is gone
The ship is at the buoy
Goodbye scarves, goodbye madras
Goodbye grain d'or, goodbye collier chou
My darling is gone
Alas, alas, it is forever

*Grain d'or and collier chou: traditional necklaces

This song, which has its roots in doudouism (a saccharine folk view of the West Indies), is attributed to François Claude Amour, marquis de Bouillé, governor of Guadeloupe from 1768 to 1771. Sung when the boats carrying men off to war would set sail, this song was still broadcast at the ports in the 1960s. The music is often played by orchestras to end a ball. The version on the recording is very well known, but there is an older one that exists:

Bonjou misyé lè gouvènè (Hello Mister Governor)
Mwen vini fè on ti pétisyon (I have come to make a plea)
Pou mandé-w lotorizasyon (To ask you for permission)
Lésé doudou an-mwen ban-mwen (To leave me my darling)
Ma dimwazèl sé byen two ta (It's much too late, Miss)

Doudou a vou ja anbaké (Your darling has already boarded the ship)
Batiman-la ja son labwé (The ship is on the buoy)
Bientôt i ké aparéyé (It is about to cast off)

The version selected is closer to the colonial view of West Indian women: losing the necklaces that the men adorn them with was more important than losing the men themselves! This song also makes reference to the traditional costume made of madras, a silk and cotton fabric native to India, whose prime accessory is the headdress.

About the language

French Creole of the Caribbean and the Indian Ocean is a relatively recent language (dating back just over three centuries) spoken by over 7 million people. With a vocabulary derived from French, at times old French, a syntax from African languages, crossed with a few Amerindian terms, it has become a language in its own right over the centuries. Nevertheless, present-day Creole still does not have a set spelling system, and several different written forms can be found depending on the author, geographic origin and cultural or historical references.

Up until the 1980s, Creole, which was often considered as "sub-French," was banned in church, on the radio, in government and especially in school. In Guadeloupe, a sign reading, "It is forbidden to speak Creole" would even be hung around the neck of a child who had broken the rule. Today, after several battles fought mainly by writers, artists and educators, attitudes are changing. Beyond its status as a language, Creole reflects the richness and history of an entire people; it abounds in linguistic treasures, and above all, embraces its oral character. Tales, fables, riddles and proverbs, but also songs, lullabies, and nursery rhymes adorn this culture of its loveliest gems.

Terms

Alèkilé: presently
Antanlontan: in the past
Batzyé: wink
Bésé ba: to bend down
Bèt a plim: bird
Dérèspékté: disrespect

Fouyaya: curious
Mouch a myèl: bee
Poux bwa: termites
Pyé bwa: tree
Tchololo: very light coffee
Zouké: to dance

Verbs are invariable. Pre-verbs indicate the tense.
Take for example, "zouké" (to dance):

Present: I ka zouké = he dances / he is dancing
Past: I té zouké = he danced
Future: I ké zouké = he will dance

Proverbs

Bwè dlo, pa néyé kyè a-w
Drink water, but don't drown your heart
(Leave some for others)

Piti vwal ka sèvi gran batiman
The small sail is useful to the large sailboat
(We often need those who are smaller than us)

Pwason adan chòdyè pa pè piman
The fish cooking in the pot is no longer
scared of the hot pepper
(When you have experienced the worst,
you have nothing left to fear)

Books

Marie-Christine Hazaël-Massieux,
Chansons des Antilles, comptines, formulettes,
L'Harmattan, 1987 (re-ed. 1996)

R. Ludwig, D. Montbrand, H. Poullet, S. Telchid,
Dictionnaire créole-français, Servedit/éditions
Jasor, 1990

C. Théodore,
Haitian Creole English — English Haitian Creole,
Hippocrene Books, 1995

Song selection, notes and vocal coordination **Chantal Grosléziat** Illustrations **Laurent Corvaisier**
Record Producer **Paul Mindy** Musical arrangement **Jean-Christophe Hoarau** and **Paul Mindy**
Recorded at **Studio Toupie** Mixed and mastered by **Philippe Kadosch** at **Multicrea** Graphic Design
Stephan Lorti for **Haus Design** and **Isabelle Southgate** Copy editing **Ruth Joseph**

SINGERS **Roselaine Bicep, Dormélia Bénédict, Josette Césarin, Marie-Paule Dantin, Paul Mindy,
Daniéla Rossignol, Dédé Saint-Prix, Lucienne Samson, Micheline Tamachia, Claudette Thégat**

CHILDREN'S VOICES **Tali Boumandil, Juliette Hoarau, Terri Samson**

MUSICIANS **Jean-Christophe Hoarau** synthesizer, guitars, banjo, bass **Paul Mindy** percussion, flute
Christine Laforêt accordion **Mario Canonge** piano **Dédé Saint-Prix** percussion, flute

TRANSLATIONS **Hector Poullet** (Haiti, Guadeloupe and Martinique) **Janick Tamachia** and **Isabelle
Pierozak** (Reunion), **Service d'édition Guy Connolly** (French to English)

AKNOWLEDGEMENTS **Marie-Christine Hazaël-Massieux, Roselaine Bicep, Micheline Tamachia,
Catherine and Patrick Halley, Daniel Hoareau, Christophe Hoareau, Eric Sidhacheety, Bazile Cléry,
Henri Poitou, Tania Chatellier, Claudine Péret, Catherine Ovide, Christophe Rosenberg,
Mireille Lamaute-Ammer, Jean-Pierre Semblat**

ⓡ **www.thesecretmountain.com**
Ⓒ ⓟ **2012 The Secret Mountain (Folle Avoine Productions)**
ISBN-10 2-923163-82-6 / ISBN-13 978-2-923163-82-6
First published in France by Didier Jeunesse, Paris, 2004